D1312008     71 5778

# DISCARD

J          Brantley, D. K.
BRA
           Every mummy has a mommy

11-12-20   CHILDREN:PICTURE BOOK

NOV 1 2 2020 778

# D.K. Brantley | Rodrigo Paulo

# EVERY MUMMY HAS A MOMMY

## Get your FREE mp3 of D.K. Brantley singing Every Mummy Has a Mommy at SirBrody.com/Mummy

Published by Sir Brody Books | Cleveland, Tennessee USA | sirbrody.com
Copyright ©D.K. Brantley, 2020 | All rights reserved
instagram.com/writebrantley | dkbrantley.com
Illustrations by Rodrigo Paulo | instagram.com/rodethos
ISBN 978-1-951551-11-7 (hardcover)

FAIRPORT PUBLIC LIBRARY
1 FAIRPORT VILLAGE LANDING
FAIRPORT NY 14450

Every mummy has a mommy,

every vampire has one too—

as does every wet,
gilled creature

living deep
in a lagoon.

This werewolf mommy
loves nuzzling

and snuggling her werewolf pup.

Frankie's mommy gives sweet kisses

first thing when Frankie wakes up.

When a young mummy feels afraid

when Creature needs
creature comfort,

it's to mommy they all go.

Boo-boos,

tummy aches,

scary dreams—

mommies care for every one.

Of all the things that mommies do

we have only just begun.

# Of course,
# dads are fantastic too.

# That fact ought not be denied.

FAIRPORT PUBLIC LIBRARY
1 FAIRPORT VILLAGE LANDING
778   FAIRPORT NY 14450

But mommies are the focus here.
So dads, please step to the side.

After years of mommy research,

the conclusion could be guessed:

Every mummy has a mommy,

CPSIA information can be obtained
at www.ICGtesting.com
Printed in the USA
LVHW071622011120
670393LV00002B/11

* 9 7 8 1 9 5 1 5 5 1 1 1 7 *